PRAISE FOR M. L. BUCHMAN

A fabulous soaring thriller.

— Take Over at Midnight, Midwest Book Review

Meticulously researched, hard-hitting, and suspenseful.

— Pure Heat, Publishers Weekly, starred review

Expert technical details abound, as do realistic military missions with superb imagery that will have readers feeling as if they are right there in the midst and on the edges of their seats.

— Light Up the Night, RT Reviews, 4 1/2 stars

Buchman has catapulted his way to the top tier of my favorite authors.

— Fresh Fiction

Nonstop action that will keep readers on the edge of their seats.

— Take Over at Midnight, Library Journal

M L. Buchman's ability to keep the reader right in the middle of the action is amazing.

— Long and Short Reviews

The only thing you'll ask yourself is, "When does the next one come out?"

— Wait Until Midnight, Romantic Times Book Reviews, 4 stars

The first...of (a) stellar, long-running (military) romantic suspense series.

— The Night is Mine, Booklist, The 20 Best Romantic Suspense Novels: Modern Masterpieces

I knew the books would be good, but I didn't realize how good.

— Night Stalkers series, Kirkus Reviews

Buchman mixes adrenalin-spiking battles and brusque military jargon with a sensitive approach.

— Publisher's Weekly

FLYING ABOVE THE HINDU KUSH

A NIGHT STALKERS ROMANCE STORY

M. L. BUCHMAN

Buchman Bookworks

Copyright 2019 Matthew Lieber Buchman

Previously published in *Fiction River Special Edition: Summer Sizzles,* 2019

Published by Buchman Bookworks, Inc.

All rights reserved.

This book, or parts thereof, may not be reproduced in any form without permission from the author.

Receive a free book and discover more by this author at: www. mlbuchman.com

Cover images:

Wakhan corridor, Afghanistan, Hindu Kush Mountains © Ninara | Flickr

Iraq Special Operations © woodfern | DepositPhotos

SIGN UP FOR M. L. BUCHMAN'S NEWSLETTER TODAY

and receive:
Release News
Free Short Stories
a Free book

Get your free book today. Do it now.
free-book.mlbuchman.com

Other works by M. L. Buchman: *(* - also in audio)*

Thrillers

Dead Chef
Swap Out!
One Chef!
Two Chef!

Miranda Chase
*Drone**
*Thunderbolt**

Romantic Suspense

Delta Force
*Target Engaged**
*Heart Strike**
*Wild Justice**
*Midnight Trust**

Firehawks
Main Flight
Pure Heat
Full Blaze
*Hot Point**
*Flash of Fire**
Wild Fire
Smokejumpers
*Wildfire at Dawn**
*Wildfire at Larch Creek**
*Wildfire on the Skagit**

The Night Stalkers
Main Flight
The Night Is Mine
I Own the Dawn
Wait Until Dark
Take Over at Midnight
Light Up the Night
Bring On the Dusk
By Break of Day
and the Navy
Christmas at Steel Beach
Christmas at Peleliu Cove

White House Holiday
*Daniel's Christmas**
*Frank's Independence Day**
*Peter's Christmas**
*Zachary's Christmas**
*Roy's Independence Day**
*Damien's Christmas**
5E
Target of the Heart
Target Lock on Love
Target of Mine
Target of One's Own

Shadow Force: Psi
*At the Slightest Sound**
*At the Quietest Word**

White House Protection Force
*Off the Leash**
*On Your Mark**
*In the Weeds**

Contemporary Romance

Eagle Cove
Return to Eagle Cove
Recipe for Eagle Cove
Longing for Eagle Cove
Keepsake for Eagle Cove

Henderson's Ranch
*Nathan's Big Sky**
*Big Sky, Loyal Heart**
*Big Sky Dog Whisperer**

Love Abroad
Heart of the Cotswolds: England
Path of Love: Cinque Terre, Italy

Other works by M. L. Buchman:

Short Story Series by M. L. Buchman:

ABOUT THIS BOOK

Night Stalkers Captain Tyra Walker *flies deep into enemy territory. It seems that flight has become her whole life's story, whether in her Arkansas hometown or in a kick-ass helicopter.*

*Delta operator **Major Norm Lawrence** stepped away from his past and only thinks about the next mission, until Tyra crosses his path.*

When Tyra's past meets Norm's present deep in the Hindu Kush Mountains—a land where military arms flow from Pakistan into Afghanistan—they'll need each other to survive the future.

1

"Okay, taking bets on who hates us more?" Captain Tyra Walker sat in the left seat of her MH-6M "Little Bird" attack helicopter and ran through engine start-up checklist called out by her copilot.

External power

Key switch

Generator Switch on

Confirm audible alarms

"Command. Definitely," her copilot Herman Geller voted in between *Gen Switch off* and *Auto Re-IGN Test switch to Test.*

"For planting us in the suck-high desert during an entire Afghan summer or for giving us the short straw of tonight's mission?" She confirmed fuel level and system-failure warning light functionality.

"I'm generous. I'm believe in Command's willingness to punish us in multiple ways. Though I'm leaning toward the latter—did you see that performance profile on this flight? *Air filter clogged warning indicator.*"

"Check." Of course she had.

Typical Command, they were loading her helo heavy, then sending her up to the theoretical limits of high-and-hot flight. Command loved the outer edge of the performance envelope. Helicopters didn't. Thin air—which only grew thinner with more altitude and the unremitting heat that was pouring sweat down the back of her neck like a tropical waterfall—gave the rotors nothing to bite on. Their Bagram Air Base hangar was almost a mile high to begin with. Where they were headed tonight was nearly double that. Heavily loaded helicopters didn't like that—not even the ones specially modified for the Night Stalkers.

"What's your vote?" she turned to her left to face Norm as he was loading his dirt bike into the helicopter's side carrier. She confirmed the cyclic-trim's motor operation, working the control beneath her right thumb and listening for the soft hum of the actuators. As always, he looked a little surprised when she addressed him directly. Maybe it was because Delta Force operators were so used to being invisible that he was uneasy at being seen.

Tonight he was the reason for an infiltrate-exfiltrate mission: deliver Norm deep into very unfriendly territory at night, hide out during the day, and then make sure he got back out the next night.

Major Norm Lawrence was anything but invisible, at least to her. Maybe because he absolutely looked the part, once she knew who he was. Delta operators weren't generally big boys like SEALs. She'd dated a SEAL or two and certainly didn't mind the way they were built one tiny bit. But Delta selected for more the wiry but tough type. The Major matched her own five-ten, and wore one-eighty of pure, lean muscle that looked damn good on him. His light tan let him blend in almost anywhere.

"My vote on what?" His voice was low and gruff, as if he rarely used it—which, being Delta, was true.

"Who hates us most tonight? We have one vote for Command, I'm in favor of the Pakis who keep supporting the Taliban while they take our aid money." She should really shut up on occasion. It sometimes felt as if she was channeling Tyra Banks "Talk Show Host", as if there hadn't been enough comparisons because they were both tall, black, and shared a name. But the other Tyra's embodiment of strength had seen Tyra herself through the toughest times so perhaps a little channeling was a good thing.

"It's just a world of joy out there," and Norm strode back toward the table to fetch more gear.

"Did a Delta just make a joke?" Geller looked up from his checklist and leaned over to stare past her at Norm's back. "He must really like you."

That pulled Tyra out of her normal routine and made her miss her reach for the collective control to lock the throttle twistgrip on Full Open.

She'd noticed Norm from the first day his small team had hit Bagram Air Base north of Kabul three weeks ago. He was impossible to miss.

Her company had flown in the day before on a huge C-5 Galaxy transport along with five of their Night Stalker helicopters. The 160th Special Operations Aviation Regiment was back in Afghanistan. They'd dragged their machines out of the plane's cargo bay and prepared them for a six-month tour. This was her third with SOAR—before that she'd flown for the 10th Mountain in Iraq. Cleaning out the Taliban and ISIL was never going to happen, but it was her job to do what she could.

The message on how painful this tour was going to be came the next day when a half dozen Delta Force operators, embedded with a platoon of fifty US Rangers, hit the pavement. In three weeks of nightly missions, this was the first time the head of the Delta team was on her bird.

Even among such a collection of fine specimens, Major Norm Lawrence had stood out. People simply made room when he walked by.

There was a buffer of respect that moved with him and few could enter it.

Over the last few weeks, they'd both taken to never passing each other without some form of acknowledgment. There was something very attractive about his self-contained nature. They'd spent an entire meal once talking about the ups and downs of being an Army Special Operations officer. Looking back, Tyra realized how exceptional that was for him. And, even more curiously, how much she'd like to do that again.

She was rarely comfortable around men—which made it God's little joke that she had ended up in the almost exclusively male world of Special Ops.

2

———

N ORM DOUBLE-CHECKED HIS GEAR THEN HAULED ON HIS pack. Only forty pounds, it felt strangely light—but tonight was recon, not assault.

Just a world of joy out there?

Shit, man!

That was the way to smooth talk a woman when she gave you an opening? Mumble something cryptic then beat ass before she had a chance to respond? He didn't want to face her response to his lame-ass remark.

He had his pick of women back Stateside. Delta bunnies were thick on the ground all around Fort Bragg, North Carolina. But Captain Tyra Walker came from a whole different class. He hadn't even known that the Night Stalkers had women pilots until he stepped off the plane and saw her. She spoke like New England Ivy League and carried herself like a runway model. As tall as he was, ballet-dancer posture, and a skin color that would get his white ass beat back home in Arkansas but looked incredible on her. There was an impenetrable reserve to her that men seemed to just bounce off—he sure as hell had.

He shifted another five pounds of ammo for his sniper rifle into his pack to have something to do—then he dumped it back out because he really didn't need it. At last the engine was fully wound up and he could see her finishing the run-up.

At the last possible second, he crossed to the Nightmare dirt bike—custom-built to Special Operations' specs—that he'd latched into the Little Bird's side carrier and climbed astride it. He snapped a line from the D-ring on the front of his vest to the helicopter's frame and pulled on the headset.

"Delta ready."

Tyra didn't even answer—which told him too much of what she thought of him. She just lifted the skids up a foot, scooted out of the hangar, and took off into the night. Within moments, the high desert terrain began shifting into the rugged foothills of the Hindu Kush Mountains. The lights of civilization were gone within minutes and the land lay black below.

He liked riding out in the wind, usually. At this temperature it was more like being desert roasted. Once Tyra hit cruise speed, he leaned against the side of the helicopter to get into the slipstream and out of the hundred-and-fifty mile-an-hour blast. He couldn't fit in the tiny rear cabin because it was filled by the ammo cases for the Minigun mounted on the tiny helicopter's other side.

His kind of ride—one with real teeth.

Like the woman at the controls—Special Operations tough.

He'd really enjoyed talking to her about serving as an officer. He could hear how deep it was in her bones despite her fine upbringing. She had ideals and had thought hard about things he'd taken for granted. She'd forced him to reflect on some of his major decisions. He'd have still ended up in the same place, but he might have done it more purposefully.

She was the first woman who'd ever forced him to think with anything above his waist.

All the Delta bunnies—actually Special Operations bunnies because the last thing a Unit operator did was admit to being *in* The Unit—didn't understand that all the low-cut dresses in the world couldn't make them soldier-hot.

At the top of his soldier-hot list was Tyra Walker, and that was before she started talking in that thoughtful way of hers.

The Little Birds flew without doors. The big windows in the doors didn't offer all that much protection and the tiny cockpits got claustrophobic fast. Plus it offered better visibility for the pilot. He could just see her left elbow as she flew. That's when he realized that he was using up the batteries in his night-vision goggles and switched them off.

Darkness descended. The thin crescent moon would be down before they reached the landing zone, only the stars lit the night—the Little Bird was blacked out. The Hindu Kush continued climbing. He'd fought in the Kunar Province before. He'd spent far too much time down in that brutal landscape and wasn't looking forward to returning. In the distance, where the Hindu Kush became the Western Himalayas, he could see the glint of snow-capped peaks—too far away to ease the pounding heat of an Afghan summer.

What would it be like to sit with Tyra, away from all this? Someplace cool and quiet where he could perhaps just talk about... That's where he ran into trouble. He was only one thing, a Unit operator. What else could he talk about that might interest a woman like her?

As if she heard him thinking about her, she spoke over the intercom.

" 'A world of joy', Major? That a pretty cheery view for a man headed into unfriendly territory," her tone was light. Perhaps he hadn't offended her and she'd merely been busy.

"Technically it's friendly territory. Pakistan is an ally."

"With allies like that..."

"...who needs enemies," he finished the old saying. She'd been thinking about his cryptic remark, which was more than he'd done before making it.

"Where's home, Major?"

"I'm not supposed to have a past. Unit operator. Man of mystery and all that."

She actually laughed.

He'd never heard her do that and it was a strangely bright sound to accompany flying into enemy country.

"Leaving a line of broken hearts behind you."

"Sure. Just dump 'em by the side of the road when I'm done. That's me. It's in the training manual."

The dull thud of descending silence shouldn't have

been audible, but it was. Now there was only the high whine of the Allison T-63 turboshaft engine, the heavy pounding of the blades, and the rush of the wind.

Shit! Teasing wasn't his style, so why did he do that? He wasn't even sure where it was coming from. Clearly it was up to him to restart this conversation—*not* one of his strengths.

"No broken hearts that I know of. And I'm from nowhere fancy. You know the movie *Winter's Bone* with Jennifer Lawrence, rural Ozarks?"

After a long silence, she came back with a careful. "I know it." Maybe she was busy with some navigation, though there was no cross-chatter with Geller.

"From there. No relation though. Jennifer Lawrence, Norm Lawrence." And, though it tasted drier than the dust in the Afghan air, he mentioned the name of his hometown. Long gone and no reason to go back.

This time the crashing silence shrouded them for over a hundred miles, crossing above the soaring peaks of the Hindu Kush Mountains to the landing site.

3

—————

"Damn you, Geller!" Tyra was almost thankful for the sudden problem as a relief from her own whirling thoughts.

"What did I do?"

"You were right," Tyra fought the controls but every time she slowed, the helo lost altitude. "Command is the one who has it in for us. What's the outside temperature?"

"One-one-five."

"How can it be a hundred and fifteen degrees at eleven at night? That's ten degrees over predicted. At present loading, that places stable hover almost a thousand feet below where I need to be." And she'd be damned if she was going to crash.

That's what had happened to the stealth bird in bin Laden's compound. Five degrees Celsius, nine Fahrenheit, *over* the predicted temperature for the raid at four thousand feet above sea level—with the helo right at its load limit including fourteen SEALs and a dog. When the air in the compound turbulated in the rotor's downwash, there was no extra lift in the rarefied air, and they went down.

And Command still hadn't learned their lesson.

"Major," it took all of the control she'd built so carefully over the years to keep her voice even. "I'm going to drop you lower down the trail and then retreat to higher ground once we're lighter."

"Roger that."

Yeah, set him down and spend who knew how many hours trying to digest an awful truth. The place she'd barely managed to escape alive, the one she'd sworn she'd never have anything to do with ever again, was the place Major Norm Lawrence called home. She was so sure she was over it, then—*Bam!*—every horrid memory slammed back to life.

Had he been friends with the guys who'd attacked her? God forbid, had he been one of them? Or the buddy who'd laughed with them afterward about the "nigger bitch" they'd nearly raped to death? Every time she heard that word now was like being thrown back into the pit.

She would *never* be ready to hear it again.

Tyra found a clearing that fit her fifty-foot minimum clearance requirements. She'd barely touched the skids to Pakistan dust before Norm—No!—before Major Lawrence was racing away. He had shed his helmet and the intercom headset for a turban and night-vision goggles. His dual mode—electric and gas—bike brilliantly illuminated the trail with an infrared headlight visible only through the NVGs.

On the ground less than five seconds, she pulled the

Little Bird up and back. Over five hundred pounds lighter, she managed to retreat and land in the planned cul-de-sac high in the mountains. She resisted the urge to fly away and leave the bastard there—barely. Within minutes, she and Geller had a camouflage net stretched over the Little Bird.

To find them now, someone would have to be hunting for them.

4

NORM WAS IN POSITION LONG BEFORE THE PRE-SUNRISE prayers.

Both the Khyber Pass far to the south and the river crossing a hundred kilometers to the north at Arandu were too well patrolled now for the munitions smugglers. It was summer, so the Pakistan merchants were desperate for safe ways to ship munitions to the insurgents in Afghanistan. During the harsh winters, the high passes were closed and there was little money until trade and crops returned each spring.

There were rumors that a new route had opened over the backbone of the border halfway between the other two crossings: from Khar, Pakistan, down the hard cliffs, and into Mangwal, Afghanistan. Khar was such a small place, he easily found a position high in the hills overlooking the square.

He unpacked and assembled his sniper rifle and wrapped it in burlap so that it wouldn't catch the light when the sun rose. His mission was strictly recon, but he needed the best view possible, which was through his sniper scope—well steadied by its attachment to the rifle. He slid on the silencer out of habit.

He lay for an hour wondering what had brought down that second comm silence during their flight. But the more he thought about it the less he understood.

Fine. He would compartmentalize it until he could ask.

Except Tyra Walker didn't compartmentalize very well. She kept sliding sideways into his thoughts in ways that were very pleasant...and horribly distracting.

After the prayers, there was movement in the square. Small tables in front of a cantina. Four men came to sit around a table.

Four men who—

Holy shit!

Three of them were Alpha targets. He'd studied the "baseball card" biographies of all the "knowns" in the area. Sitting down for morning coffee were: the leader of Kunar Province Taliban, the Number Two in Afghanistan's branch of ISIL, and a Pakistani general known to be corrupt as hell. The last, whoever he was, was not likely to be a good guy. Guards lounged around the square, their AK-47s on clear display. Any villagers with an ounce of common sense would be far away.

Recon only.

But they didn't train Delta to make decisions slowly or fail to modify plans as needed. This was a kill-list opportunity like few he'd ever heard of. He'd didn't have the forces to take them prisoner and get intel, but he could certainly damage the beast.

He eased out his satellite radio and called Command. Was a drone available? Yes there was one in the area. Authorization? Answer promised in five minutes. Good thing it was still early evening in Washington DC. Once a politician called it a night they were useless.

He kept his eye on the target. If they started to leave, he'd take them down with or without authorization. Twelve hundred meters, three quarters of a mile, but within range of his weapon...barely.

5

Tyra sat among the boulders on the dirt. She had to get away from the helicopter. Even from Geller whose turn it was to be on watch. She and Herman had flown together for over a year now, so he knew that her silence was out of the ordinary and she damned well wouldn't be explaining herself to him either.

She had left the past behind. Far behind. After all, it was a decade ago.

She'd been with men since then and congratulated herself on being clear of the baggage. How had it followed her through time and halfway around the world? The therapist had warned her all those years ago that it might and she'd set out to prove him wrong. What did a *man* know about rape survivors? Apparently too much.

Tyra had made it a mission to redefine herself, her life...and she had the perfect image to use. *Tyra Banks Supermodel of the Year.* First African-American on the cover of GQ and twice *Sports Illustrated* Swimsuit Issue cover. Smart too. Her own show. Her own everything.

Tyra Walker had done the same, except it had been her version. She'd—

A sharp crack of gunfire sounded behind her.

She spun and raised the FN-SCAR rifle that always hung across every Night Stalker's chest and sighted back toward the Little Bird just as Geller's body tumbled out of the helicopter to the ground. No living man would fall in such a way.

Not the time to think about him.

The assailant was on the far side of the helo, but she could see his legs under the belly.

She didn't hesitate to kneecap him.

He didn't fall—she'd have killed him if he did— though his scream was very satisfying. A quick scan. Only one. Some lone scout who had heard her when she'd flown too low last night and had come looking.

Then something came flying over the helo in her direction.

A grenade, headed right for her in a perfect lob. There was no way to dive clear, no rock to get behind that wouldn't expose her to fire.

She counted seconds.

A trained soldier held a grenade long enough so that it exploded as it reached the target. The average person wanted to get rid of a live grenade as fast as they can.

Out of choices, Tyra bet her life on the assailant being average.

One one thousand.

Two one thousand.

Three—

She caught it high and, spinning her arm, winged it back low and hard. It wasn't her best pitch, but she'd been a top softball pitcher before…well, before.

Four one thousand.

It bounced once in the dirt beneath the helicopter and arrived at the assailant's feet just at fi—

She dove behind her small boulder as the grenade blew. A few bits of shrapnel pinged the rocks around her.

Then she peeked around the side of her shield.

Big mistake!

She saw the leading edge of the fireball and barely managed to escape it.

A Little Bird's fuel tanks were crash-rated not to leak. However, blowing up a grenade right below a tank had been too much.

The fuel touched off and blew the shit out of her Little Bird. No little pings of shrapnel—this time whole chunks of her helicopter crashed around her.

Pilot's seat.

A piece of the motorcycle carrier.

A twist of composite that might have once been a rotor blade.

Her helmet, that she'd left on her seat, ricocheted off multiple rocks like a pinball in a life-sized game.

The fireball roared aloft as the helo burned.

Then the ammunition for the Minigun began exploding. Most of it wasn't going anywhere, but eight thousand rounds of 7.62x51mm ammo went up far faster than even a Minigun could fire them. All Tyra could do was cover her ears and pray.

6

Norm heard the thump even though he was a dozen kilometers away. At first he thought his airstrike had arrived and somehow hit behind him. Then he turned and saw the roiling tower of smoke far back in the mountains.

There was only one thing up in those hills that could explode like that: Tyra's helicopter.

A scathing, whispered, curse didn't make him feel any better. He couldn't leave until—

Authorization for an airstrike or not, time was up. He lined up the shot, then had to wait until he could get his racing pulse rate back under control... There.

One, Two, Three—the radio squawked—Four.

Four bullets in flight before the first one had time to arrive.

He sent four more, bracketing their targets' likely movements as the first rounds drove home.

He grabbed the radio.

"Strike authorized. Lase target." He didn't have time for this, but he also didn't have a choice.

He flicked on the infrared laser that hung under the barrel and held it on the center of the table. Three were down, one was crawling away.

He shifted his aim, but there was no need.

A Hellfire missile slammed down and obliterated the village square. The buildings to all sides lost roofs, two even had their front walls blown in.

The guard details were all down as well. Any civilian casualties would be up to the village and the news media to deal with. Delta Force, as invisible as always, had nothing official to do with this kill.

The radio was squawking at him, but it wasn't Tyra so he ignored it.

He sprinted the three hundred meters back to where he'd stashed the bike, moving faster than any Super Bowl running back with a wide-open field before him.

The electric engine gave him a near-silent departure for the first kilometer. Then he fired off the gas engine and opened the throttle wide.

7

Tyra was lost. The black hole had swallowed her.

Once again she was face down in the ditch. Naked. Broken.

That horrific night she hadn't seen anything except the headlights of the truck that pulled up behind her. She'd run out of gas while trying to get home from the Running Start program at the community college during her high school senior year. Nothing but the flashlight in her face when the bad Samaritans came up beside her car.

Later, afterward, Tyra had crawled along the ditch to escape the blazing heat of the car they'd torched. Her mother's car. Vague memories of lying in the hospital bed while her mother screamed. Blaming her for not watching the gas gauge. More upset about the destruction of her eight-year-old Dodge than of her daughter. Even half conscious, Tyra had known she herself was done with her past.

The rape kit testing had revealed five men's DNA,

none on record. She'd lost count, but it had seemed like more. Maybe the test was crap.

Tyra could only cower as the cop had found her, lost and broken beside her mother's precious burning—

A hand touched her and she screamed.

"It's okay, Tyra. It's me."

The look in her eyes told him that she had no idea who he was.

"It's Major Norm Lawrence. It's okay. I'm here now."

He reached for her again, but she scrambled away.

"Don't you dare touch me!"

Then he was staring down the wrong end of an FN-SCAR combat assault rifle. She knelt in a textbook firing position. The safety was off, her finger was inside the trigger guard, actually on the trigger. It was rock steady in her hands—her response time was worthy of a Unit operator. At ten feet there wasn't a chance she'd miss.

Norm backed off. Held his hands open.

"It's okay. We have to get out of here. Now."

"Not. With. You."

Had she blown up her own helicopter? Gone somehow rogue, or insane? That didn't seem likely or he'd be dead already.

He glanced at the still burning wreckage. The whole

upper part of the helicopter was gone, shredded, but parts of the belly still remained upright on the skids.

Beyond it, he could see a body...no, two. One wore a Night Stalkers survival vest even though he was burned beyond recognition. The other was a native, or at least parts of one—as attested to by the half-melted AK47. A quick scan of the surroundings, but they were alone for now. Just one local fighter. It wouldn't stay that way for long.

Moving as fast as he dared under Tyra's tracking aim, he circled the wreckage.

Nothing to salvage.

Even the Night Stalker in the vest was unrecoverable except for a femur here and a hand there. He grabbed a bag from the bike and collected what he could, which was little enough. He did find the dog tags blown twenty feet away, but if the man had a "last letter" in his pocket, it was long gone. Norm couldn't even remember Geller's first name.

"We need to move now," he circled back around to Tyra who still had her rifle up. Her finger outside the trigger guard now, but he still wouldn't be able to outdraw her.

"I repeat: not with you."

"You know who I am?"

"Yes, and I know where you're from. And I was almost killed there by a bunch of your Ozark buddies. I'm sure they told you grand stories in the bar—it's not that big a town." Her voice sliced through the heat with a chill deeper than a Hindu Kush winter.

"When?" He could see her breathing rate. If she didn't

slow it down soon she was going to hyperventilate, even at this altitude.

"Ten years ago."

"I left fifteen ago. I've never been back."

"Do you swear?" Tyra's voice was still brittle.

He laid his hand on his heart and the sudden move made her flinch. Bad choice. "On my honor as an officer."

Norm counted ten beats of his heart beneath his hand while she stared at him with those dark eyes, gone almost black. She finally shifted her aim aside, but remained on her knees.

Then she hung her head and sat still as death.

"Tyra?"

She nodded once, twice. Then using her rifle like a crutch, she managed to reach her feet, but her shoulders remained hunched, cringing as if the world would strike her at any moment.

No, as if *he* would.

Unsure what else to do, he pulled his sidearm out and held it out to her butt first.

She stared at his weapon, then slowly, finally, looked up at his eyes.

"Take it. If it will make you feel safer, take it." He felt strange offering it. He'd fired tens of thousands of rounds with this weapon in training. It had been his companion through hundreds of missions. Yet he couldn't think of what else to do.

She studied the weapon again, then shook her head.

He reholstered it, slowly. "Can we go now?"

Tyra looked up and scanned the horizon as if aware of her surroundings for the first time. She nodded. He led her to the bike. It wouldn't be long before someone came looking to see what had happened here.

He dropped the bag of Geller's remains into a saddlebag. From the other, he took a trio of breaching charges—each big enough to take out a heavy steel door. A second explosion wasn't going to draw any more attention. Besides, this one would be small and smokeless.

Hurrying now, he arranged them around the last of Geller's gear. He tossed a few bits and pieces of the helo, those that had survived total destruction, on top. He trotted back to the bike and flipped a trigger.

There was a hard thump—nothing bigger than his palm remained. That was the best he could do.

He swung onto the bike, then looked at Tyra who stood just two paces away.

9

Climbing onto the back of the dirt bike and lacing her hands into the sides of Norm's vest might count as the hardest thing Tyra had ever done.

Every place she touched him—and it wasn't that big a bike—had her twitching with nerves and cold sweat despite the heat.

Thankfully he didn't ask if she was ready, because there was no way she could have answered.

The ride was a blur.

The rear wheel skidded along the trail as Norm laid hard into corners. He took them south and west into the depths of the Hindu Kush.

The packed-dirt road thinned to a porter's trail, probably for mules. Norm turned off it onto a goat track, and then led them deeper into the mountains until they were making their own way across bare rock and weaving between boulder fields.

Somewhere along the way, finally feeling she was just

maybe safe, she lay her forehead against the back of his vest and wept.

For Herman Geller who had always been a bright spot in any mission.

She wept for the innocence of the girl who'd been driving down the road singing along to country-western on the radio when she ran out of gas.

She wept for the past that hadn't been purged. Could never be purged.

And finally she'd wept simply because she'd needed to.

She was barely conscious of Norm carrying her out of the heat and into a shallow but blissfully cool cave. While she sipped from the bottle of water he'd put in her hands, he radioed in their location. A helo would come for them after dark. The drone was retasked to keep an eye out for anyone approaching their remote position.

Finally, he settled beside her, his back against the same cave wall as hers. His rifle lay in his lap, pointing at the entrance. Their view was wide and covered the only possible approaches across the rocky ground.

"Why did you leave your home?" Tyra's voice was barely a whisper.

10

———

Norm had been starting to wonder if she'd ever speak again.

"It was a small town. Didn't like it much. My dad was a big man who spoke with his fists. Which had taught Mom not to speak at all. Even at school I was the misfit. Didn't care enough about to learn much from the teachers, too small for football, did okay in baseball. I liked third base, a real action spot. But never got close to anyone. After high school, I simply walked out, hitched a ride to the nearest recruiter's office, and asked to be let in."

It all seemed so simple now, even if the steps hadn't been nearly that orderly. He told her about going Rangers, Officer Candidate School, then Delta tapping him for testing—one of the great honors of his life, even if he hadn't fully understood that until now. The Unit only recruited the best.

It was like that one dinner they'd shared, explaining things to Tyra brought them into focus.

"The Unit is as close to home as I ever imagined."

"And now?" Her voice still too quiet to even echo in the cave.

He shrugged. "Told you. I'm not that much of a thinking guy. Except when you're around it seems. What about you?" And then— "Shit! Sorry. Ignore that question. I'm thinking you've had enough of the past for one day."

"I've had enough of the past to last a lifetime." Her laugh was a scoff but, however rough, it was still a laugh. Then a deep sigh. "You probably need to know, I was a victim of rape, in your—" her voice nearly strangled with tightness, "—in *our* hometown."

"Did they catch the bastard?" A fury surged through him worse than watching his father beat his mom, he himself already too battered to fight back.

"No. And I don't think they ever will. The cops tried, but I never saw their faces."

" 'Their'?" *Shit!* If he ever found them he'd—

A cool hand rested briefly over his. "Thank you for that."

"For what?" He couldn't keep the snarl out of his voice.

"Over the years I've learned the hard way that some guys are put off by a woman who's been violated. Some sickos are turned on by it. Still others go blank as if I never spoke, as if it didn't matter. You're pissed. That emotion sustained me for a long time...once I climbed out far enough to get there."

"Climbed out far enough? Tyra, you climbed out so far the hole filled in behind you and a forest grew over it.

I had you pegged for some hot model with a Princeton education or one of those other posh schools up north. Just couldn't figure out why the hell you were a Night Stalker instead of off somewhere being famous or something."

"I'm a Night Stalker because it's important. I discovered that I like to fight back and I'm damned good at it."

Which he'd seen for himself. They sat in silence for a long time while Norm tried to shift his view of the woman beside him. He just couldn't make Southern girl fit. But now he couldn't make her Northern fit either.

She was...herself.

And that was truly incredible.

11

———

"Is that why you wouldn't talk to me? Thinking I was all stuck-up Ivy League?" Tyra often was told that she was, but it was wrong. She was protecting herself. Holding up a shield against a past. One that maybe —*please let it be true*—finally couldn't touch her anymore.

"No," Norm smiled. "No. I didn't talk to you much because you scare the shit out of me. So goddamn beautiful and smart. Then add being a SOAR officer on top of that... You are an amazing package."

"I'm an amazing *woman*," and she felt an utterly womanly sigh at the way he saw her. As the person she'd spent so many years trying to become. Maybe the past was truly over— No! Maybe the past was, at long last, truly *in* the past.

"Right, that's what I meant," Norm finally turned away from the scorched landscape beyond the cave's mouth and looked at her.

"I forgot that for a while after the explosion," and she

could still feel the hole and knew it would always be there. But Norm was right. It *was* filled in and grown over. She'd finally flown high enough to climb clear of it, even if she could never be wholly free. She couldn't leave the past completely behind, because that too was a part of who she was.

"You *are* an amazing woman," his face suddenly Delta-serious. "You better keep remembering that. Every day!" Like he was handing out marching orders.

"I do." And those words echoed strangely inside her. Not because they were foreign, but rather because one day, with this man, they could be so very right.

He raised an arm in question and she didn't hesitate to answer by sliding through his protective shield just as he had slipped through hers.

That feeling was itself an answer. Whatever her past, Norm was a amazing man who wasn't a part of it. Now their mutual protective defense wrapped them together rather than driving them apart. They sat hip to hip, their rifles in their laps, and before them an incredible vista of the jagged Hindu Kush Mountains. But they were the brutal past.

Beyond the cool warmth of their cave, the achingly blue sky beckoned her ever upward.

When Norm kissed her on the temple, their course shone as clear as a flight plan. Together they were going to fly so high.

———

If you enjoyed this, keep reading for an excerpt from a book you're going to love.
..and a review is always welcome (it really helps)...

IF YOU ENJOYED THIS, YOU'LL LOVE THE NIGHT STALKERS 5E

TARGET OF THE HEART (EXCERPT)

Major Pete Napier hovered his MH-47G Chinook helicopter ten kilometers outside of Lhasa, Tibet and a mere two inches off the tundra. A mixed action team of Delta Force and The Activity—the slipperiest intel group on the planet—flung themselves aboard.

The additional load sent an infinitesimal shift in the cyclic control in his right hand. The hydraulics to close the rear loading ramp hummed through the entire frame of the massive helicopter. By the time his crew chief could reach forward to slap an "all secure" signal against his shoulder, they were already ten feet up and fifty out. That was enough altitude. He kept the nose down as he clawed for speed in the thin air at eleven thousand feet.

"Totally worth it," one of the D-boys announced as soon as he was on the Chinook's internal intercom.

He'd have to remember to tell that to the two Black Hawks flying guard for him...when they were in a friendly country and could risk a radio transmission. This deep inside China—or rather Chinese-held territory as the CIA's mission-briefing spook had insisted on calling it —radios attracted attention and were only used to avoid imminent death and destruction.

"Great, now I just need to get us out of this alive."

"Do that, Pete. We'd appreciate it."

He wished to hell he had a stealth bird like the one that had gone into bin Laden's compound. But the one that had crashed during that raid had been blown up. Where there was one, there were always two, but the second had gone back into hiding as thoroughly as if it had never existed. He hadn't heard a word about it since.

The Tibetan terrain was amazing, even if all he could see of it was the monochromatic green of night vision. And blackness. The largest city in Tibet lay a mere ten kilometers away and they were flying over barren wilderness. He could crash out here and no one would know for decades unless some yak herder stumbled upon them. Or were yaks in Mongolia? He was a corn-fed, white boy from Colorado, what did he know about Tibet? Most of the countries he'd flown into on Black Ops missions he'd only seen at night anyway.

While moving very, very fast.

Like now.

The inside of his visor was painted with overlapping readouts. A pre-defined terrain map, the best that modern satellite imaging could build made the first layer. This wasn't some crappy, on-line, look-at-a-picture-of-your-house display. Someone had a pile of dung outside their goat pen? He could see it, tell you how high it was, and probably say if they were pygmy goats or full-size

LaManchas by the size of their shit-pellets if he zoomed in.

On top of that were projected the forward-looking infrared camera images. The FLIR imaging gave him a real-time overlay, in case someone had put an addition onto their goat shed since the last satellite pass or parked their tractor across his intended flight path.

His nervous system was paying autonomic attention to that combined landscape. He also compensated for the thin air at altitude as he instinctively chose when to start his climb over said goat shed or his swerve around it.

It was the third layer, the tactical display that had most of his attention. At least he and the two Black Hawks flying escort on him were finally on the move.

To insert this deep into Tibet, without passing over Bhutan or Nepal, they'd had to add wingtanks on the Black Hawks' hardpoints where he'd much rather have a couple banks of Hellfire missiles. Still, they had 20 mm chain guns and the crew chiefs had miniguns which was some comfort. His twin-rotor Chinook might be the biggest helicopter that the Night Stalkers flew, but it was the cargo van of Special Operations and only had two miniguns and a machine gun of its own. Though he'd put his three crew chiefs up against the best Black Hawk shooter any day.

While the action team was busy infiltrating the capital city and gathering intelligence on the particularly brutal Chinese assistant administrator, Pete and his crews had been squatting out in the wilderness under a camouflage net designed to make his helo look like just another god-forsaken Himalayan lump of granite.

Command had determined that it was better for the helos to wait on site through the day than risk flying out and back in. He and his crew had stood shifts on guard duty, but none of them had slept. They'd been flying together too long to have any new jokes, so they'd played a lot of cribbage. He'd long ago ruled no gambling on a mission, after a fistfight had broken out about a bluff hand that cost a Marine three hundred and forty-seven dollars. Marines hated losing to Army no matter how many times it happened. They'd had to sit on him for a long time before he calmed down.

Tonight's mission was part of an on-going campaign to discredit the Chinese "presence" in Tibet on the international stage—as if occupying the country the last sixty-plus years didn't count toward ruling, whether invited or not. As usual, there was a crucial vote coming up at the U.N.—that, as usual, the Chinese could be guaranteed to ignore. However, the ever-hopeful CIA was in a hurry to make sure that any damaging information that they could validate was disseminated as thoroughly as possible prior to the vote.

Not his concern.

His concern was, were they going to pass over some Chinese sentry post at their top speed of a hundred and ninety-six miles an hour? The sentries would then call down a couple Shenyang J-16 jet fighters that could hustle along at Mach 2—over fifteen *hundred* mph—to fry his sorry ass. He knew there was a pair of them parked at Lhasa along with some older gear that would be just as effective against his three helos.

"Don't suppose you could get a move on, Pete?"

"Eat shit, Nicolai!" He was a good man to have as a copilot. Pete knew he was holding on too tight, and Nicolai knew that a joke was the right way to ease the moment.

He, Nicolai, and the four pilots in the two Black Hawks had a long way to go tonight and he'd never make it if he stayed so tight on the controls that he could barely maneuver. Pete eased off and felt his fingers tingle with the rush of returning blood. They dove down into gorges and followed them as long as they dared. They hugged cliff walls at every opportunity to decrease their radar profile. And they climbed.

That was the true danger—they would be up near the helos' limits when they crossed over the backbone of the Himalayas in their rush for India. The air was so rarefied that they burned fuel at a prodigious rate. Their reserve didn't allow for any extended battles while crossing the border...not for any battle at all really.

———

It was pitch dark outside her helicopter when Captain Danielle Delacroix stamped on the left rudder pedal while giving the big Chinook right-directed control on the cyclic. It tipped her most of the way onto her side but let her continue in a straight line. A Chinook's rotors were sixty feet across—front to back they overlapped to make the spread a hundred feet long. By cross-controlling her bird to tip it, she managed to execute a straight line between two mock pylons only thirty feet apart. They were made of thin cloth so they wouldn't down the helo if you sliced one—she was the only trainee to not have cut one yet.

At her current angle of attack, she took up less than a half-rotor of width, just twenty-four feet. That left her nearly three feet to either side, sufficient as she was moving at under a hundred knots.

The training instructor sitting beside her in the copilot's seat didn't react as she swooped through the training course at Fort Campbell, Kentucky. Only child of a single mother, she was used to providing her own feedback loops, so she didn't expect anything else. Those who expected outside validation rarely survived the SOAR induction testing, never mind the two years of training that followed.

As a loner kid, Danielle had learned that self-motivated congratulations and fun were much easier to come by than external ones. She'd spent innumerable hours deep in her mind as a pre-teen superheroine. At twenty-nine she was well on her way to becoming a real life one, though Helo-girl had never been a character she'd thought of in her youth.

External validation or not, after two years of training with the U.S. Army's 160th Special Operations Aviation Regiment she was ready for some action. At least *she* was convinced that she was. But the trainers of Fort Campbell, Kentucky had not signed off on anyone in her trainee class yet. Nor had they given any hint of when they might.

She ducked ten tons of racing Chinook under a bridge and bounced into a near vertical climb to clear the power line on the far side. Like a ride on the toboggan at

Terrassee Dufferin during *Le Carnaval de Québec,* only with ten thousand horsepower at her fingertips. Using her Army signing bonus—the first money in her life that was truly hers—to attend *Le Carnaval* had been her one trip back to her birthplace since her mother took them to America when she was ten.

To even apply to SOAR required five years of prior military rotorcraft experience. She had applied after seven years because of a chance encounter—or rather what she'd thought was a chance encounter at the time.

Captain Justin Roberts had been a top Chinook pilot, the one who had convinced her to switch from her beloved Black Hawk and try out the massive twin-rotor craft. One flight and she'd been a goner, begging her commander until he gave in and let her cross over to the new platform. Justin had made the jump from the 10th Mountain Division to the 160th SOAR not long after that.

Then one night she'd been having pizza in Watertown, New York a couple miles off the 10th's base at Fort Drum.

"Danielle?" Justin had greeted her with the surprise of finding a good friend in an unexpected place. Danielle had always liked Justin—even if he was a too-tall, too-handsome cowboy and completely knew it. But "good friend" was unusual for Danielle, with anyone, and Justin came close.

"Captain Roberts," as a dry greeting over the top edge of her Suzanne Brockmann novel didn't faze him in the slightest.

"Mind if I join ya?" A question he then answered for himself by sliding into the opposite seat and taking a slice of her pizza. She been thinking of taking the leftovers back to base, but that was now an idle thought.

"Are you enjoying life in SOAR?" she did her best to appear a normal, social human, a skill she'd learned by rote. *Greeting someone you knew after a time apart? Ask a question about them.* "They treating you well?"

"Whoo-ee, you have no idea, Danielle," his voice was smooth as...well, always...so she wouldn't think about it also sounding like a pickup line. He was beautiful but didn't interest her; the outgoing ones never did.

"Tell me." *Men love to talk about themselves, so let them.*

And he did. But she'd soon forgotten about her novel and would have forgotten the pizza if he hadn't reminded her to eat.

His stories shifted from intriguing to fascinating. There was a world out there that she'd been only peripherally aware of. The Night Stalkers of the 160th SOAR weren't simply better helicopter pilots, they were the most highly-trained and best-equipped ones anywhere. Their missions were pure razor's edge and Black Op dark.

He'd left her with a hundred questions and enough interest to fill out an application to the 160th Special Operations Aviation Regiment (airborne). Being a decent guy, Justin even paid for the pizza after eating half.

The speed at which she was rushed into testing told her that her meeting with Justin hadn't been by chance and that she owed him more than half a pizza next time they met. She'd asked after him a couple of times since she'd made it past the qualification exams—and the examiners' brutal interviews that had left her questioning her sanity, never mind her ability.

"Justin Roberts is presently deployed, ma'am," was the only response she'd ever gotten.

Now that she was through training—almost, had to be soon, didn't it?—Danielle realized that was probably less of an evasion and more likely to do with the brutal op tempo the Night Stalkers maintained. The SOAR 1st Battalion had just won the coveted Lt. General Ellis D. Parker awards for Outstanding Combat Aviation Battalion *and* Aviation Battalion of the Year. They'd been on deployment every single day of the last year, actually of the last decade-plus since 9/11.

The very first Special Forces boots on the ground in Afghanistan were delivered that October by the Night Stalkers and nothing had slacked off since. Justin might be in the 5th battalion D company, but they were just as heavily assigned as the 1st.

Part of the recruits' training had included tours in Afghanistan. But unlike their prior deployments, these were brief, intense, and then they'd be back in the States pushing to integrate their new skills.

SOAR needed her training to end and so did she.

Danielle was ready for the job, in her own, inestimable opinion. But she wasn't going to get there until the trainers signed off that she'd reached fully mission-qualified proficiency. FMQ was the gold star of the Night Stalkers pipeline.

The Fort Campbell training course was never set up the same from one flight to the next, but it always had a time limit. The time would be short and they didn't tell you what it was. So she drove the Chinook for all it was worth like Regina Jaquess waterskiing her way to U.S. Ski Team Female Athlete of the Year.

The Night Stalkers were a damned secretive lot, and after two years of training, she understood why. With seven years flying for the 10th, she'd thought she was good.

She'd been repeatedly lauded as one of the top pilots at Fort Drum.

The Night Stalkers had offered an education in what it really meant to fly. In the two years of training, she'd flown more hours than in the seven years prior, despite two deployments to Iraq. And spent more time in the classroom than her life-to-date accumulated flight hours.

But she was ready now. It was *très viscérale,* right down in her bones she could feel it. The Chinook was as much a part of her nervous system as breathing.

Too bad they didn't build men the way they built the big Chinooks—especially the MH-47G which were built specifically to SOAR's requirements. The aircraft were steady, trustworthy, and the most immensely powerful helicopters deployed in the U.S. Army—what more could a girl ask for? But finding a superhero man to go with her superhero helicopter was just a fantasy for a lonely girl who'd once had dreams of more.

She dove down into a canyon and slid to a hover mere inches over the reservoir inside the thirty-second window laid out on the flight plan.

Danielle resisted a sigh. She was ready for something to happen and to happen soon.

————

PETE'S CHINOOK AND HIS TWO ESCORT BLACK HAWKS crossed into the mountainous province of Sikkim, India ten feet over the glaciers and still moving fast. It was an hour before dawn, they'd made it out of China while it was still dark.

"Thirty minutes of fuel remaining," Nicolai said it like a personal challenge when they hit the border.

"Thanks, I never would have noticed."

It had been a nail-biting tradeoff: the more fuel he burned, the more easily he climbed due to the lighter load. The more he climbed, the faster he burned what little fuel remained.

Safe in Indian airspace he climbed hard as Nicolai counted down the minutes remaining, burning fuel even faster than he had been while crossing the mountains of southern Tibet. They caught up with the U.S. Air Force HC-130P Combat King refueling tanker with only ten minutes of fuel left.

"Ram that bitch," Nicolai called out.

Pete extended the refueling probe which reached only a few feet beyond the forward edge of the rotor blade and drove at the basket trailing behind the tanker on its long hose.

He nailed it on the first try despite the fluky winds. Striking the valve in the basket with over four hundred pounds of pressure, a clamp snapped over the refueling probe and Jet A fuel shot into his tanks.

His helo had the least fuel due to having the most men aboard, so he was first in line. His Number Two picked up the second refueling basket trailing off the other wing of the Combat King. Thirty seconds and three hundred gallons later and he was breathing much more easily.

"Ah," Nicolai sighed. "It is better than the sex," his thick Russian accent only ever surfaced in this moment or in a bar while picking up women.

"Hey, Nicolai," Nicky the Greek called over the intercom from his crew chief position seated behind Pete. "Do you make love in Russian?"

A question Pete had always been careful to avoid.

"For you, I make special exception." That got a laugh over the system.

Which explained why Pete always kept his mouth shut at this moment.

"The ladies, Nicolai? What about the ladies?" Alfie the portside gunner asked.

"Ah," he sighed happily as he signaled that the other helos had finished their refueling and formed up to either side, "the ladies love the Russian. They don't need to know I grew up in Maryland and I learn my great-great-grandfather's native tongue at the University called Virginia."

He sounded so pleased that Pete wished he'd done the same rather than study Japanese and Mandarin.

Another two hours of—Thank God—straight-and-level flight at altitude through the breaking dawn and they landed on the aircraft carrier awaiting them in the Bay of Bengal. India had agreed to turn a blind eye as long as the Americans never actually touched their soil.

Once standing on the deck—and the worst of the

kinks had been worked out—he pulled his team together: six pilots and seven crew chiefs.

"Honor to serve!" He saluted them sharply.

"Hell yeah!" They shouted in unison and saluted in turn. It was their version of spiking the football in the end zone.

A petty officer in a bright green vest appeared at his elbow, "Follow me please, sir." He pointed toward the Navy-gray command structure that towered above the carrier's deck. The rear admiral of the entire carrier strike group was waiting for him just outside the entrance. Not a good idea to keep a one-star waiting, so he waved at the team.

"See you in the mess for dinner," he shouted to the crew over the noise of an F-18 Hornet fighter jet trapping on the #2 wire. After two days of surviving on MREs while squatting on the Tibetan tundra, he was ready for a steak, a burger, a mountain of pasta, whatever. Or maybe all three.

The green escorted him across the hazards of the busy flight deck. Pete had kept his helmet on to buffer the noise, but even at that he winced as another Hornet fired up and was flung aloft by the catapult.

"Orders, Major Napier," the Rear Admiral handed him a folded sheet the moment he arrived. "Hate to lose you." He saluted, which Pete automatically returned before looking down at the sheet of paper in his hands. The man was gone before the import of Pete's orders slammed in.

A different green-clad deckhand showed up with Pete's duffle bag and began guiding him toward a loading

C-2 Greyhound twin-prop airplane. It was parked Number Two for the launch catapult, close behind the raised jet-blast deflector.

His crew, being led across in the opposite direction to return to the berthing decks below, looked at him aghast.

"Stateside," was all he managed to gasp out as they passed.

A stream of foul cursing followed him from behind. Their crew was tight. Why the hell was Command breaking it up?

And what in the name of fuck-all had he done to deserve this?

He glanced at the orders again as he stumbled up the Greyhound's rear ramp and crash landed into a seat.

Training rookies?

It was worse than a demotion.

This was punishment.

Keep reading at fine retailers everywhere.
Target of the Heart
...and don't forget that review. It really helps me out.

ABOUT THE AUTHOR

M.L. "Matt" Buchman started the first of over 60 novels, 100 short stories, and a fast-growing pile of audiobooks while flying from South Korea to ride his bicycle across the Australian Outback. Part of a solo around the world trip that ultimately launched his writing career in: thrillers, military romantic suspense, contemporary romance, and SF/F.

Recently named in *The 20 Best Romantic Suspense Novels: Modern Masterpieces* by ALA's Booklist, they have also selected his works three times as "Top-10 Romance Novel of the Year." NPR and B&N listed other works as "Best 5 of the Year."

As a 30-year project manager with a geophysics degree who has: designed and built houses, flown and jumped out of planes, and solo-sailed a 50' ketch. He is awed by what's possible. More at: www.mlbuchman.com.

Other works by M. L. Buchman: (* - also in audio)

Thrillers

Dead Chef
Swap Out!
One Chef!
Two Chef!

Miranda Chase
*Drone**
*Thunderbolt**

Romantic Suspense

Delta Force
*Target Engaged**
*Heart Strike**
*Wild Justice**
*Midnight Trust**

Firehawks
MAIN FLIGHT
Pure Heat
Full Blaze
*Hot Point**
*Flash of Fire**
Wild Fire

SMOKEJUMPERS
*Wildfire at Dawn**
*Wildfire at Larch Creek**
*Wildfire on the Skagit**

The Night Stalkers
MAIN FLIGHT
The Night Is Mine
I Own the Dawn
Wait Until Dark
Take Over at Midnight
Light Up the Night
Bring On the Dusk
By Break of Day
AND THE NAVY
Christmas at Steel Beach
Christmas at Peleliu Cove

WHITE HOUSE HOLIDAY
*Daniel's Christmas**
*Frank's Independence Day**
*Peter's Christmas**
*Zachary's Christmas**
*Roy's Independence Day**
*Damien's Christmas**
5E
Target of the Heart
Target Lock on Love
Target of Mine
Target of One's Own

Shadow Force: Psi
*At the Slightest Sound**
*At the Quietest Word**

White House Protection Force
*Off the Leash**
*On Your Mark**
*In the Weeds**

Contemporary Romance

Eagle Cove
Return to Eagle Cove
Recipe for Eagle Cove
Longing for Eagle Cove
Keepsake for Eagle Cove

Henderson's Ranch
*Nathan's Big Sky**
*Big Sky, Loyal Heart**
*Big Sky Dog Whisperer**

Love Abroad
Heart of the Cotswolds: England
Path of Love: Cinque Terre, Italy

Other works by M. L. Buchman:

<table>
<tr><td>

Contemporary Romance (cont)

Where Dreams
Where Dreams are Born
Where Dreams Reside
Where Dreams Are of Christmas
Where Dreams Unfold
Where Dreams Are Written

</td><td>

Science Fiction / Fantasy

Deities Anonymous
Cookbook from Hell: Reheated
Saviors 101

Single Titles
The Nara Reaction
Monk's Maze
the Me and Elsie Chronicles

Non-Fiction

Strategies for Success
Managing Your Inner Artist/Writer
*Estate Planning for Authors**
Character Voice
Narrate and Record Your Own
*Audiobook**

</td></tr>
</table>

Short Story Series by M. L. Buchman:

<table>
<tr><td>

Romantic Suspense

Delta Force
Delta Force

Firehawks
The Firehawks Lookouts
The Firehawks Hotshots
The Firebirds

The Night Stalkers
The Night Stalkers
The Night Stalkers 5E
The Night Stalkers CSAR
The Night Stalkers Wedding Stories

US Coast Guard
US Coast Guard

White House Protection Force
White House Protection Force

</td><td>

Contemporary Romance

Eagle Cove
Eagle Cove

Henderson's Ranch
Henderson's Ranch

Where Dreams
Where Dreams

Thrillers

Dead Chef
Dead Chef

Science Fiction / Fantasy

Deities Anonymous
Deities Anonymous

Other
The Future Night Stalkers
Single Titles

</td></tr>
</table>

SIGN UP FOR M. L. BUCHMAN'S NEWSLETTER TODAY

and receive:
Release News
Free Short Stories
a Free Book

Get your free book today. Do it now.
free-book.mlbuchman.com

www.ingramcontent.com/pod-product-compliance
Lightning Source LLC
Chambersburg PA
CBHW032051180726
48284CB00004B/1292